Once there was a little girl called Mia, who came from a city of streetlights and stars.

But Mia left her home, with its cooing pigeons and rumbling trains, and came to live with her Grandma, deep in the heart of a whispering forest.

Grandma Mitzi had hair as silver as birch trees and skin that smelt of lavender. Her voice was as warm as sunshine, but Mia hardly knew her.

"This is your new room and all the toys are for you," said Grandma Mitzi. Mia looked around but didn't touch anything. She wasn't used to the quiet wooden house or the whispers of the forest.

"And this is Lucky," smiled Grandma Mitzi.
Mia gazed into Lucky's big brown eyes.
She had never had a pet before.

"And this is the forest," said Grandma Mitzi as they tramped past enormous trees. Mia felt frightened of the strange silvery shadows. Then suddenly she saw something twinkling like a star. It fluttered through the air and landed on her nose.

"It's cold!" she gasped.

"It's snow!" laughed Grandma Mitzi.
"Snow!" breathed Mia, and she
chased the twirling flakes all
the way to the village school.

"You'll be coming here next term," said Grandma Mitzi softly.
Mia stared at the children, as pale as snow, so different from
the children in the city.

A girl in a blue coat looked up and waved. Mia's heart gave
a little skip. Perhaps this girl will be my friend, she thought.

But Mia felt too shy to wave
back, so she followed Lucky
back through the forest.

When they got home,
Grandma Mitzi lit a fire and
made a big pot of steamy soup.
But Mia just nibbled at
a piece of bread and
stroked Lucky's silky fur.

She lay in her bed, too restless to dream. Everything is so different, she thought. And then she remembered the moon.

"You're the same moon that shines over the city!" Mia gasped.

She pulled on her red coat and ran outside to see her moon.

When Mia reached the garden, she stood quite still, for the world had turned magical. A million snowflakes floated through the air, each one as rare and beautiful as a star.

And through the dark night, Mia thought she heard the winter wind whisper a song of ice and starlight:

"Every snowflake is different, every snowflake is perfect."

And Mia realised that it didn't matter how different she felt, she was perfect too. And she smiled a smile as bright as her moon.

The next morning, Grandma Mitzi said,
"Today is a special day. All the children hang
winter decorations on the oldest tree in the village."

Mia stared at the other families, so different from hers, and suddenly she felt lost.

But then three snowflakes fell
from the clouds and brushed
her skin like kisses.

Every snowflake is different,
every snowflake is perfect,
thought Mia, and she walked
a little closer to the tree.

"My name is Ava," said the girl in the blue coat. "What's your name and where do you come from?"

"My name is Mia and I came with the snow," said Mia, and she hung a red heart on a branch of the tree.

"Do you want to come sledging?" asked Ava, and she took Mia's hand and they ran through the snow together.